# TINA

## The Really Rascally Red Fox

# VeraLee Wiggins

# TINA
## The Really Rascally Red Fox

# VeraLee Wiggins

**Pacific Press® Publishing Association**
Nampa, Idaho
Oshawa, Ontario, Canada

# Other Books in the Julius and Friends Series

Julius

Julius Again

# Dedication

I wish to dedicate this book to its author, VeraLee Wiggins who passed away on December 24, 1995 at the age of 67. She was my beloved wife, constant companion, and best friend for 50 years. She loved animals and spent many hours caring for the little orphan fox in this story.

Leroy Wiggins

Edited by Jerry D. Thomas
Designed by Dennis Ferree
Cover art by Mary Rumford
Inside art by Linda Hawkins
Typeset in New Century Schoolbook 14/17

Library of Congress Cataloging-in-Publication Data:
Wiggins, VeraLee, 1928-1995

    Tina  :  the really rascally red fox  /  VeraLee Wiggins ;
[illustrated by Linda Hawkins].
      p.   cm.
    Summary:  While caring for her orphaned pet fox, Sara
learns to love all of nature's creatures and the God who
created them.
    ISBN  0-8163-1321-0  (alk. paper)
    [1. Foxes. 2. Pets. 3. Christian life.]  I. Hawkins, Linda, ill.
II.  Title.
PZ7.W6386Ti   1996
[Fic]—dc20                                   95-52409
                                               CIP
                                             AC

04 05 06 07 • 5 4 3 2

# Contents

*Sara tucked the crying baby fox
under her chin and they both
went back to sleep.*

# CHAPTER

# 1

# A Baby Surprise

"Hi, Sara. I'm bringing home a surprise tonight."

Sara could tell by the sound of her dad's voice that something exciting was going on. She held the telephone tight against her ear, and her heart beat faster. "What is it, Dad?"

He chuckled. "If I told you, it wouldn't be a surprise, would it? You tell the rest of the family so you can be ready, OK?"

Sara said goodbye and ran outside where her mom and her little brother Derek played croquet. "Your turn, Sara," Mom called, handing her the green mallet.

Sara nudged the green ball, easing it through

the wicket. "That was Dad on the phone," she said, sounding excited. "He's bringing home a surprise."

Four-year-old Derek jumped up and down. "What is it, Sara? What's the surprise?"

"If he told us what it is, it wouldn't be a surprise," Sara said, in exact imitation of Dad.

The afternoon dragged by, but at last Dad walked through the door. He laid something tiny, wrapped in a soft cloth, on the couch. A moment later, it moved! Everyone crowded close while Sara pulled the cloth away. A tiny furry gray animal squirmed on the soft cushion, struggling to stand on its weak little legs.

"A puppy! Can I hold it?" Derek yelled.

Dad shook his head and smiled. "Don't shout. You'll scare the little baby. And it isn't a puppy, Derek."

Three pairs of eyes fastened on Dad's face, waiting to learn what kind of helpless little animal he'd brought home.

Dad smiled gently. "It's a baby fox. One of my clients brought it in this afternoon. He found it on his farm."

Mom, the animal lover, stiffened up. "Wade!" she said sternly. "You know better than to kidnap baby animals. We'll just take it right back to the farm."

Dad shook his head again and looked sad. "He watched the baby for two days. No mother appeared, and it's very weak. He was on the way to the Humane Society to have it put to sleep when I rescued it."

Mom's eyes softened, and she picked up the little fox. Ever so gently, she examined it. Tears crowded into her blue eyes but didn't run over. "This little thing can't be over two weeks old. Somebody hurt its mother and dumped the baby." She handed it to Sara. "Hold it against you so it feels safe. I'll fix some milk."

Sara followed Mom to the kitchen, carefully carrying the baby fox. "May I help?"

"Sure. Go into the bathroom and find a new medicine dropper," Mom said, opening the refrigerator.

Mom had a warm milk mixture ready when Sara returned. Sara eased herself into a rocker, holding the baby's head up. Mom pushed the tip of the dropper into the tiny mouth and squeezed. When the baby tasted the warm milk, it began sucking hard, making loud slurping noises. It choked several times as it tried to drink. Mom filled the dropper three times. "That's enough for a first time," she said, looking much happier. "We'll do it again in an hour."

The whole family helped with supper. After they finished the dishes, they all marched in to check on the new baby. The fox, wrapped in its little blue cloth, slept soundly on the couch.

"Well," Mom said, laughing as she rocked Derek. "I guess we really needed another family member. We only have two kids, two cats, and a dog."

"You're right, Jenny," Dad said. "Two kids, two spoiled Siamese cats, and one old—very old—collie dog." He ran a big hand through his blond hair and grinned sheepishly. "We really didn't need another pet."

Sara looked at the tiny bundle on the couch, and her heart tried to pound a hole in her chest. "I'll take care of it, Mom," she promised. "School will be out in two weeks; then I'll do everything. You won't even know we have a fox.

The fox whimpered, so Sara ran after its milk. It sucked several teaspoons from the dropper again, then closed its eyes and laid its head on Sara's hand.

"I want to hold it," Derek announced.

Sara laid the miniature fox against Derek's chest. "Put your hand on its back," she said, "and be very careful."

"I thought foxes were bigger," Derek said as he petted the fox and looked it over. "This one is tiny."

Dad shook his head. "I've never seen a fox this young before, so I don't know if this one is smaller than usual. If it lives, we'll see how big it grows."

"I don't care if it's small, Daddy. I like our new pet," Derek said, petting the furry little back. The fox coughed, so Sara took it and held it to her shoulder.

That night at worship time, Mom explained that the baby fox was much too young to take from its mother, and it might not live. She added that it was really bad to keep a wild animal, that it wanted to be free. But this one would have died if someone hadn't helped it.

"Something bad happened to its mother all right," Dad said, "or we would never, ever have bothered it." Then everyone prayed for the tiny fox to be all right. Sara made a soft little bed in a box beside her bed. She fed the baby, put it into its bed, and hopped into her own. Her eyes had barely closed when she heard a tiny little sound.

"*Mmmmm mmmmm mmmmm.*"

Struggling out of bed, she heated some more milk, but the baby wouldn't take it this time. Sara put it back to bed, but it cried again, louder, and coughed.

Sara felt too tired to care for a crying baby, so she pulled it into her bed and snuggled it under her chin. The fox settled down, and Sara dropped into a sound sleep.

"*Mmmmmm mmmmm mmmmm.*"

Sara forced herself to wake up. *I wonder what time it is*, she thought as she heated milk. A look at her watch told her. *Eleven-thirty! I've only been asleep for an hour!* The fox drank two teaspoons of milk, and Sara tucked it under her chin again. They both slept.

The baby awakened every hour for milk, then slept under Sara's chin.

The next morning, Sara barely heard Mom's cheery wake-up call.

"Mom," she whimpered, when she finally crawled from her warm bed, "I only got forty-five minutes' sleep every hour. I can't go to school."

Mom laughed. "Now you know how I felt

when you and Derek were small. Sometimes you didn't let me get even that much sleep."

Sara went to school, but she could hardly wait for the bus to stop at her house that afternoon. "How's the baby, Mom?" she yelled, dumping her books on the hall floor.

Mom met her before she reached the living room, shaking her dark head. "I'm afraid it's sick, Sara. It's coughing a lot. I have an appointment at the vet's in half an hour. Want to come?"

Sara did!

After examining the tiny animal, Dr. Reuben raised his black eyebrows and smiled. "Your fox has pneumonia (new-moan-e-uh), but thanks to some good medicine, she'll be all well in a few days."

Sara's spine tingled as she watched the doctor tear the paper off a hypodermic needle, fill it with some white stuff, and stick it into the helpless little fox's neck.

*Tina, the Really Rascally Red Fox*

# CHAPTER

## 2

# Tina Meets the Siamese Cats

Sara could hardly stand it when the doctor stuck the needle into the baby fox's neck. The tiny animal didn't seem to notice the shot at all. Dr. Reuben smiled. "I saw that look on your face, Sara. Do you know why shots hurt?"

Sara shook her head.

"I know," Derek said importantly. "Because they make a hole in your skin." He nodded his blond head for emphasis.

Dr. Reuben laughed. "No, Derek, they're so sharp you don't even feel them go into your skin. They hurt because you tense up, and the needle has a hard time getting through those hard muscles. The fox didn't know she was getting a shot, so she relaxed. And it didn't hurt her. She didn't jump or cry, did she?"

Derek and Sara both shook their heads.

Dr. Reuben handed Mom some medicine in a bottle. "I want you to put half a dropper of this in each feeding."

Mom nodded. "All right. How often should we feed the fox—and what?"

"Feed her when she cries. I'll give you a formula and a little bottle with a soft nipple. She should be bright and sassy in less than a week." He turned to Sara. "This fox is very young, so it won't be doing much of anything for some time. What it needs right now is a nice, warm place where it can feel secure. I doubt if it can even walk yet."

"He can't," Derek informed him. "He can only crawl, and his tummy drags."

The vet winked at Derek. "Your fox is a little girl, Derek. And she'll be walking soon."

Back home, Mom gave Sara some old towels, which she made into a warm nest. She put the baby in and covered her with more towels. The fox cuddled down and stopped whining.

Dad came home from the office in a little while, and they all sat down at the table for supper. "How's the fox?" Dad wanted to know after Derek asked the blessing.

"It's sick, Daddy, but it will get better," Derek answered, his blue eyes wide.

Dad looked at Mom. She nodded. "It has pneumonia, but Derek's right. The vet gave her a shot and some medicine. He said she'll soon be well."

"The vet told us she's a girl too, so let's find a name for her," Sara added eagerly.

Dad messed up Sara's brown curls. "OK. We will need something to call her when she starts getting into everything around the place."

"Call her Tiny," Derek said. "She's smaller than a kitten."

"The vet said she weighs seven ounces," Sara said. "That's less than half a pound."

"How about Teensie?" Derek asked.

"How about Minnie?" Mom suggested. "She's only as big as a minute."

"No," Derek and Sara chorused. "That's a mouse's name." Everyone tried to think of a good name for the fox as they ate the delicious vegetable soup and hot rolls Mom had made.

"Tina!" Sara said, when they finished eating. "Her name is Tina. I read somewhere that

'Tina' means 'tiny' in Spanish."

"I like Tina," Derek echoed.

"Tina sounds good to me," Mom said. She looked at Dad with a question in her eyes.

Dad nodded, smiling. "Sure. Our fox will like Tina, even when she isn't tiny anymore."

Mom mixed up the milk as Dr. Reuben had told her and showed Sara how to add the medicine. Tina slept in her little bed all evening, only waking once to be fed.

At worship that night, Sara could hardly wait for her turn to pray. "Thank You, God, for giving us our special pet," she said. "Help her to get well quick. Help us to take good care of her until she's old enough to be on her own." Derek copied Sara's prayer except he prayed that Tina would never be wild again.

Sara undressed happily that night. *I'm so glad Tina feels better tonight*, she prayed silently as she slipped between the cool sheets. *Help her to have a good night's sleep. We're both ready for a nice, long rest. Thank You, Father*.

But she didn't even get her eyes shut before she heard the tiny cry. "*Mmmmmm mmmmm mmmmm*." Then Tina coughed. Sara hopped out of bed. She heated the milk and medicine and poured it into the little bottle to feed the hungry fox.

After carefully cleaning the bottle, Sara tucked the towels all around the fox, hopped into bed, and closed her eyes. She was so tired, and her bed felt so nice.

"*Mmmmmm mmmmm mmmmm.*"

Sara scooped the tiny animal from its bed and cuddled it under her chin. She tucked the covers tight around them and fell asleep.

Sometime later, a tiny cough awakened Sara, and she took care of the baby, then climbed back into her warm bed. She didn't put Tina back into her box but cuddled her close. Both enjoyed a long rest.

Tina stayed in her little nest box during the days for the next two weeks, except when she could coax someone to cuddle her. At night, Sara never put her in the box. Tina always slept with her. She knew the fox would sleep better, and so would she.

After a few days, Tina stopped coughing, and her fur started to shine. Then she began trying to escape from the box. "Let's leave her in the box until she learns to climb out," Mom said.

Sara agreed. "Yes, she's so tiny something could happen to her. But she has grown. Could we weigh her somehow?"

Mom got out the food scales. They found a light little box and put Tina in it on the scales. "Hey, she weighs 13 ounces now," Sara said. "She's almost doubled her weight."

One evening as the family ate supper, Dad started laughing. He pointed to the family room.

A tiny gray animal sniffed around, checking out the big world.

"Well, so much for keeping her in a box," Sara said as she held and petted the little fox after supper. After a moment, she put the fox on the floor.

"Do you have your fox house-trained yet?" Dad asked, wearing a smug grin.

"Oh no! What are we going to do?" Mom wailed.

"I guess I go around after her with a napkin," Sara said.

"Get a litter box," Derek said.

Dad rubbed his chin. "I don't know, son. A fox is a wild animal."

"I think he has a good idea," Mom said. "At

least worth trying. I'll get some litter in the morning."

At that moment, the Siamese cats strolled into the family room and spotted Tina. Their backs arched, and their black tails grew to twice their natural size.

Tina saw the cats and flattened herself on the carpet, hoping the cats wouldn't see her.

Dad grinned and pointed at the cats and fox. "Watch this," he mouthed to Sara.

The cats watched the tiny animal a moment, then stuck their black noses into the air and sniffed. Seeming satisfied, their tails smoothed down, and they advanced step by step toward Tina.

"Tina's so flat she looks like a rug," Derek said.

The cats got about two feet from the fox, stopped, and sniffed again.

*Tina ran right up Sara's back
and jumped off her head!*

# CHAPTER

# 3

# Tina's a Little Stinker!

When the cats got close enough to sniff Tina, a strong odor filled the room. The cats' tails grew big again. Spinning away from the fox, they raced from the room. "Wow, I'm going too," Derek said. He ran outside through the sliding-glass door.

"What is it?" Sara asked, barely able to handle the horrible smell.

"It reminds me of a skunk, but different, somehow," Mom said.

Sara scooped the trembling fox into her arms, then quickly put her on the floor again. "It's Tina!" she said. She ran to the bathroom and washed her hands and arms.

When Sara returned to the family room, Dad laughed at her. "I opened the window and glass door," he said. "I think your little "skunk" had an accident. Better give her a bath."

Sara bathed the fox with the baby shampoo Mom used on Derek. Tina's smell sickened Sara, but someone had to bathe her. At least Tina behaved almost as though she enjoyed the cleaning.

"Did she come out smelling like a rose?" Dad asked, after Sara gave Tina a good brushing.

"No, but it was a big improvement," Sara said. "What happened, Dad? Why did she smell like that?"

Dad showed Sara the big encyclopedia. "I just read a little about foxes. They have musk glands similar to skunks, though not nearly as strong. Really, Sara, they do. It says due to these glands, foxes don't make very good pets. I guess we know what it means, don't we?"

"So what are you saying? I can't keep her anymore?"

Dad shook his head. "What would we do with her? She needs us now. But we'll have to be careful not to scare her or make her mad."

The next morning, Mom and Sara fixed up

a litter box and put Tina in it. The tiny animal smelled every inch of the kitty litter, turned around twice, and made a little puddle.

"Good girl!" Mom said. She petted and cuddled the pleased little animal.

Sara put Tina in the litter box every hour. The baby fox used it each time. Sara poured on the praise, and Tina never had an accident after that.

Sara added canned dog food to Tina's diet, and she grew even faster. Her gray blue eyes began to change to the bright amber that would be their adult color.

One day Sara took her pet outside, leaving the sliding-glass door open a few inches. Tina watched and chased butterflies hovering over the petunia garden at the back of the lawn.

Sara lay on a quilt on the lawn watching her baby trying to catch the teasing, twisting insects. Suddenly Tina stopped short, held her head high, then turned and ran as fast as she could up the concrete steps into the house and straight to her litter box. A moment later, she jumped out of the box and trotted back to Sara. She had a proud look in her eyes, as though she were saying, "It was tough, but I made it."

"I think you understood exactly what we want," Sara said, petting Tina's silky head. "You don't have to be quite that well litter-box trained. It would be perfectly all right for you to potty outside, you know."

The months passed quickly, and Tina turned into a beautiful, half-grown vixen (a female fox). Her coat lightened into a reddish gold, and her legs lengthened. She could outrun Sara and enjoy doing it. The Donovan family left the sliding glass door open a few inches all the time so Tina could go in or out to please herself.

"Sara, the garden needs to be weeded today," Dad said one morning at the breakfast table.

"Oh, Dad, why do I have to do everything?" Sara whined. "Can Derek help?"

Dad smiled and tugged a lock of Sara's dark hair. "Sure. But it will be your responsibility to keep him from taking out the vegetables. Maybe Tina will eat the insects while you and Derek chop out the weeks."

"Come on, Derek, we have to weed the garden," Sara yelled, after Dad drove off to work.

Derek came running. "Did Daddy say I could weed, Sara? Did he?"

Sara shook her head. Imagine wanting to weed. "Come on, I'll show you."

Sara pulled several weeds. "See, Derek? These are weeds. They all look different from each other." She handed him a weeder, which was only a paring knife with its end bent sideways. She pointed to the beans. "These things that are all alike are beans. Don't week them out, OK?"

"OK."

Sara took the row beside Derek's, and they crawled on their hands and knees, working with their weeders. Suddenly, she felt something run up her legs onto her back. Before she had time to get excited, Tina ran onto her head and jumped off onto the soft earth in front of her. After falling on her face, the playful animal picked herself up and took off running.

"Hey, did you see that?" Derek yelled. "Tina jumped off your head!"

"I know," Sara said. "I felt it." She returned to her work and pulled a few weeds. Then she felt the quick little feet scamper over her again. The fox paused on Sara's head, then jumped a little farther than the first time.

"This is fun!" Derek said. "Make her jump off my head, Sara."

"I can't make her do anything," Sara said. "She may not do it to me anymore."

But every little while, all morning, Tina ran up Sara's back, paused, and jumped off her head. She never did it to Derek, though he wanted her to in the worst way.

"She's playing a game," Sara explained as the fox jumped from her head, circled back, and repeated the performance. "She thinks my head is her diving board."

Tina wandered away and entertained herself chasing butterflies for a while, then returned to her jumping game. One time she ran up Sara's back, stopped short, then turned and scrambled back the way she came. Sara watched her little pet run for the house as fast as she could go until she disappeared through the sliding door.

"She had to go potty," she told Derek.

"We should take the litter box outside," Derek said.

"Good idea," Sara said. "How did you get so smart?"

After they had the garden weeded, Sara moved the litter box outside. "I'll just put it here on the patio for now," she said. "In a few days, I'll move it a little farther out."

Tina still slept with Sara every night. Not in a box beside the bed. Not on top of the covers at the foot of the bed. She slept under the covers, crowding close to Sara all night.

One Sunday morning, Sara awakened to find Tina gone. Jumping out of bed, she still didn't see her pet. So she decided to take a quick shower. When she returned from the bathroom, she found her fox on a chair. But what was Tina lying on?

Sara gently lifted her little friend off her silky yellow church dress. *I better hang that up, or it'll be all wrinkled*, Sara thought. She snatched the dress from the chair and started to straighten it, but a sleeve fell to the floor.

The sleeve had been chewed from the dress— and the rest of the dress had more holes than a big slice of Swiss cheese!

*Tina, the Really Rascally Red Fox*

# CHAPTER

*4*

## Tina Eats a Dress

*What will Mom say when she sees this?* Sara could just imagine. "I've asked you over and over to hang up your clothes when you take them off, Sara. Will you never learn?"

Sara opened her closet door, shoved the dress into a dark corner, and slammed the door. Then she shook her head. *I can't do that. Mom will find out anyway, and I don't want to try to trick her.* She yanked the door back open and grabbed the ruined dress. Tucking it under her arm, she headed for the kitchen. Tina ran happily at her heels.

"Hello," Mom sang out when Sara walked into the kitchen. She glanced down at the prancing fox. "You girls look great this morning."

Sara held the ruined dress behind her back. "Sometimes people aren't as good as they look," she said.

"Oh, oh, I recognize that look," Mom said. "What's the problem?"

Sara didn't know how to answer. She pulled out the dress and laid the mess on the table.

Mom picked it up and looked at it; then her eyes dropped to the playful little animal on the floor. Finally her blue eyes met Sara's. "It was a really pretty dress, but wasn't it getting too short for you?"

*What! She's not mad?* Sara couldn't believe her ears. "Mom! It fit just fine."

Mom glanced once more at the shredded dress. She shook her head, then smiled brightly. "I'm sorry, Sara, but the dress is gone. I'm sure your little pet is worth it."

Sara ran to her mother and gave her a giant hug. "Thanks, Mom. You're the only mother in the whole world who would say that." Sara went away thinking about what a marvelous mother she had. *Mom could have screamed her head off about Tina wrecking the dress. We don't have the money to be buying new dresses all the time. Thank You, God, for giving me the parents you did.*

Tina grew fast. Soon she neared her full size. Her coat turned a shiny red gold, but her feet remained black. And she wanted to go everywhere Sara did.

One day Mom, Sara, and Derek returned from a shopping trip. Tina met them in the driveway and ran back and forth and around them as fast as she could run, whining all the time.

"It's a good thing we came home," Derek said. "Tina missed us."

Sara squatted down, and the crazed fox jumped into her arms, wiggling all over. "Right," Sara said. She turned to Mom. "But have you noticed she never wags her tail? Never, no matter how happy she is?"

Mom smiled and petted the happy little animal. "Aren't you forgetting something?" she asked.

"Forgetting what?"

Mom's eyes twinkled. "Tina isn't a dog. She doesn't slobber all over your face, either."

That night, Dad seemed to have something

funny on his mind. Every little while he giggled. "Tell us, Daddy," Derek insisted. "We want to laugh too."

"Are you sure, son?" Dad asked, mussing Derek's blond hair."OK, I checked a Spanish dictionary today, and guess what *Tina* means?"

"Sara said it means 'a little fox,' " Derek said.

"I did not," Sara said, laughing. "I said it means 'little.' "

Dad smiled quietly. "Well, according to the dictionary I have at the office, *Tina* means 'ringworm of the scalp or beehive spider.' The very best I could come up with was 'a large jar or tub.' " He laughed some more.

"That's not very funny, Dad," Sara said. "What are we supposed to do? Tina has known her name for a long time."

"Don't change it. I've seen that fox go through dog food. Even though she's not fat, I'd call her a tub."

That night when Tina cuddled close in bed, Sara said, "I love you, no matter what you are, my little tub." Tina wiggled all over.

"Mommy, can I build a treehouse in the oak tree?" Derek asked one morning while he and

Sara ate breakfast.

Mom looked up from the camera she'd been studying. "Aren't you a little small for such a big job?"

Derek's large blue eyes sparkled, and his lips turned into a trusting smile. "Sara will help me."

Sara liked the idea too. "Dad, if Derek and I really do want to build a treehouse in the oak grove, what wood could we use?"

Dad rubbed his chin. "We have some good trees for one, but I don't remember any lumber lying around."

"I do," Mom said. "What about that wood stacked up behind the church. Last week they asked for a volunteer to haul the stuff away. Why couldn't they use that lumber?"

"Hey, I saw that stack last Sabbath," Sara said. "We'll just pick out some good boards and carry them over." They made a few trips during the afternoon, and by evening, there was a big pile of boards piled at the bottom of the largest oak tree.

As they tried to figure out where to start, Mom called to them from the boysenberry garden. "Sara, have you and Derek been into the berry patch? There are hardly any berries here, and the vines have been torn."

Sara shook her head, "We've been working all afternoon."

Derek's blue eyes turned toward the golden collie lying on the lawn. "Maybe Duke got hungry."

Mom glanced at the old dog. "Dogs don't eat berries, honey. Well, let's go in and put supper on the table." Mom shook her small pan of berries. "A bowl of fresh boysenberries would have been so good for supper."

Tina met them at the door with a purple face. "Here's the berry thief, Mom," Sara said. "Tina, you bad little girl. You stole our supper. And don't you know foxes don't eat berries?"

After supper, Tina crawled into Sara's lap while she read. Then Sara noticed Tina's feet! Thorns and bloody scratches covered her black pads. "Tina, those boysenberry bushes really got the best of you. Was it worth it?" Sara began gently picking out the thorns.

Dad came into the family room and watched Sara working on Tina. "You like her a lot, don't you?" he said, looking pleased.

Sara nodded, returning his big smile. "She's

a neat pet, Dad. And she's never smelled bad since that night she met the cats."

"That's because she hasn't been upset."

"I'll just have to make sure she stays happy, then."

Dad watched Sara picking out one black thorn after another from the little black pads. "Have you ever thought about God's kindness?" he asked. "Making so many special things for us to enjoy?"

Sara nodded. "Like Tina."

Dad grinned. "Yes, like Tina." He chuckled and winked at Sara. "And boysenberries," he added. "Something else I think about is how He heals our scratches and bruises. If He didn't heal us, we'd end up looking look like an old dented car."

"True," Sara said, still picking thorns from Tina. "I guess every time a sore heals, God has just done a little miracle for us, hasn't He?"

Then Sara remembered the boards beside the big oak. "Hey, Dad, how do I build a treehouse?"

Dad heaved himself from the chair. "Looks like you're finished with Tina. Why don't we go have a look?" Tina ran out with them but soon got bored and left.

"Hey, this is going to be great," Dad said. He gave a long jump and pulled himself into the leafy tree. "I'll help you do it Sunday if you can wait that long."

Sara felt relieved. "Super! I don't even know how to start."

Just then, Duke's growl and low bark sounded from the backyard, followed by several high yaps.

"Something's happened to Tina," Sara yelled. She took off running toward the house. "Hurry, Dad," she called over her shoulder.

*Tina pounced on Duke's tail.*
*But she was in for a surprise!*

# CHAPTER

# 5

# A Thief in the Neighborhood

Sara and Dad ran to the edge of the lawn and stopped. "Look," Sara whispered.

The seventeen-year-old collie lay on the lawn, trying to sleep. The little fox pounced at his tail, yapping and nipping at the long hair on the end. As they watched, Duke got slowly to his feet and tried to chase Tina. But Tina zipped around him and nipped at his tail again before the old dog completed his slow-motion attack. Then Duke turned around to charge the fox again, but by that time, Tina had run to his other end and hung on to his tail again.

"I'm going to help Duke," Dad said, starting to move. But two flashes of tan and black caught Tina by surprise. The Siamese cats! Cindy landed on the fox's head, and Dusty piled onto her back.

Tina forgot all about the old collie and ran in circles on the lawn yapping. The cats didn't say anything. They just kept riding the fox as though they did it every day.

Then Tina spotted Sara and headed for her. Dad put his hand over his mouth to keep from laughing out loud as Tina shot between Sara's legs. Both cats tumbled off and disappeared into the wide flower garden behind the lawn.

"Phew!" Dad said, holding his nose. He ran ten feet from the fox. "Your skunk lost control again," he said, grinning.

Sara lifted the stinking fox into her arms and ran to the house. "I hope you learned something, you rotten little thing." She put the smelly animal into the bathtub. "I'll clean you up this time, but you'd better be good from now on, OK?"

That night, Tina sat on Sara's lap, as she always did, during family worship. Sara absently ran her fingers through Tina's long, sweet-smelling fur.

After they finished prayer, Dad leaned back.

"God cares for the helpless, doesn't He? I don't think those cats especially like Duke, but God sent them to rescue him, didn't He? What a marvelous Father we have." He reached over and petted Tina's back a little.

When Dad drew his hand back, Tina looked into Sara's eyes, climbed to her shoulder, and draped herself around Sara's neck.

Mom looked at the relaxed animal and laughed. "I always said I'd never wear a fur or let any of my family wear one. I have to admit, though, yours looks good."

Sunday morning, Dad, Derek, and Sara hurried to the oak grove to work on the treehouse. As soon as they had a sturdy six-by-eight-foot floor built, Dad hoisted Derek up so he could help. They attached boards to the sides until they had walls about five feet tall with windows in each side of the house. They put on a slanted roof with more of the old Dorcas building boards.

"Rain will come through this roof, Daddy," Derek said. "I can see blue sky right through it."

Dad agreed. "OK, kids, let's get the mower."

Sara pushed the mower across the large, grassy field. Then Dad raked up the dry grass.

Derek helped mix the water and dirt. Two hours later, a mixture of mud and grass covered the roof of the treehouse. "Now take a look at the ceiling," Dad said to Derek.

Derek looked around. Then he jumped up and down in the house that nestled high in the tree. "It's a super terrific house now," he yelled.

"Now, we'll have to nail boards on the side of the tree to climb up and down on," Dad said.

Derek pointed to a long, low limb leaning down almost to the ground. "We don't need a ladder on the tree, Daddy. We can climb up on that limb."

Dad gave the limb a quick look. "That limb won't hold you guys." He stuck some nails in his mouth and began nailing sturdy boards to the tree, about a foot apart. "OK, son, come see if you can climb into your treehouse," he said when he finished.

Derek scrambled up the board steps in a flash. He leaned out the treehouse window. "It works fine, Daddy."

Tina sat at the foot of the tree, looking up at Derek, yapping as fast as she could open and shut her mouth.

"OK, Tina, let's go." Sara grabbed her pet

and ran up the ladder with her. She dropped Tina onto the floor of the house, and the fox ran in circles, looking the place over. She sniffed every board she could reach. When satisfied that she knew every inch of the new house, she propped her front feet on the window and watched Dad walking back to the house.

"Thanks, Dad," Sara called after him. "Tina likes the house too."

Sara turned around to discover that Dusty and Cindy had arrived from somewhere.

The cats walked all over the treehouse too, sniffing out all the interesting smells. Tina crouched in the corner away from the cats. "This place is getting crowded," Sara said. Picking up the fox, she climbed down the ladder.

Derek and Sara carried several things out to the treehouse in the next few days—a small radio, an old record player and old records, and some quilts and pillows.

"Are you guys moving out there?" Dad asked.

Derek's face brightened. "Can we?"

Sara shook her head. "No way, Derek. We can play there in the daytime, but forget sleeping out there."

Several days later, Derek came to Mom. "I

can't find my shoes. I put them in the garage because they got dirty."

"You better find them," Mom said absently, looking up from her photography lesson book. "No new shoes for Derek until fall."

But he didn't find them.

The next day at breakfast, Mom asked Sara and Derek to weed the garden. "I think it will be the last time this year," she said.

Sara enjoyed weeding now, because she knew Tina would play her "Jump Off Sara's Head" game. She hadn't finished her first row when the little animal ran up her back, onto her head, then took a flying leap. She landed skidding, then ran in a circle, came up behind Sara, and did it again. And again. And again.

"I wish I could do that," Derek said. "Can I do it, Sara?"

"Derek, you're not a fox," Sara said, tossing her sweater onto the lawn. "And you're much too heavy. You would mash me into the ground."

Finally, Derek and Sara stood up and dusted themselves off. "Thanks for helping, Derek," Sara said. "I'm glad that's finished for the year, even though Tina will miss it."

"Hey, look!" Derek yelled, pointing to the

open area past the lawn. Tina ran through the mowed-off dry grass. Every little while she jumped four feet straight into the air, as though she were on springs. Then she would trot along a few feet and go straight up again. "What's she doing?" Derek asked.

"Let's go see." They crept closer to the fox and watched. "She's catching grasshoppers," Sara said a few minutes later.

Sara and Derek watched, fascinated. Even seeing, it was hard to believe. Tina ran smoothly through the dried grass. Suddenly, she sprang four feet in the air, still in running position. Each time, she snapped a grasshopper and dropped to the ground running.

The next morning, Sara felt cool and looked around for her sweater. "Mom, did you pick up my sweater?" she asked.

"No, Sara. You're old enough to pick up your own clothes. Where did you leave it?" Sara couldn't remember and soon gave up the search. The sun was getting warm, anyway.

The next day, the cat-food dish disappeared. Then Mom left a weeder in the flower garden while she ate lunch. When she went back, it seemed to have sprouted legs and walked off.

*Tina, the Really Rascally Red Fox*

# CHAPTER

# 6

# Dad Tackles Tina!

"Somebody's stealing everything that isn't nailed down around here," Dad said when Sara complained about losing a book. She had left it on a quilt in the back lawn.

"I can remember when nobody ever worried about leaving things lying around," Mom said.

"I know," Dad replied, "but things are different in this day and age. We better start being extra careful about locking the house too. I would hate to come home and find everything stolen."

"Wait a minute, Dad," Sara said. "Do we lock Tina out or in? We always leave the patio door open for her."

Dad smiled grimly. "The cats got along before we left the door open. I guess the fox can too. She knows the place now and isn't afraid of anything."

"I guess we can try her out tonight," Mom said. "This is our evening to go see Grandma and Grandpa."

Sara showered and put on clean jeans and a shirt. *What am I going to do with Tina?* she thought. *She'll really think we hate her if she can't go in and out to please herself. And you never know, something could happen to her. Hey! She could go with us!*

Surprisingly, Mom and Dad agreed, so the family took off in the station wagon with Tina draped around Sara's neck.

Grandma laughed when she saw Sara's fox decoration. "I declare, Sara, I never thought you'd wear fur."

"Let's sit in the backyard," Grandpa said. "Your fox might get frightened inside." He grinned. "And from what I hear, I don't want her to get upset in my house!"

The little group sat in lawn chairs in the shady backyard. Tina snooped around, smelling each plant in the flower beds as well as every inch of the weathered board fence. Every little while, she ran to Sara to make sure everything was all right, then returned to her snooping.

All at once, Sara shrieked. Two lively dogs had appeared from nowhere and, ears raised, trotted into the backyard. "Help, quick," Sara called, "let's chase the dogs out of here." The tall board fence completely enclosed Grandma's backyard, so the dogs had to be herded toward the open gate.

But the dogs spotted Tina and set up a howl that old Duke could have heard at home. Tina dashed the length of the fence. She ran with her nose close to the bottom of the boards, looking for a way to escape.

Then she spotted the open gate. She stuck her tail straight out behind, lowered her nose, and headed for the gate like a Fourth of July rocket.

The two dogs hit the trail behind Tina. A moment later, all three animals disappeared through the gate and around the corner. The dogs howled as if they had treed a cougar.

Dad was only a few seconds behind the dogs. After a moment of shocked silence, Sara shot through the gate too. Seeing Dad halfway down the block, she followed, running fast.

The noisy, fast-moving group raced another block, across the street, turned to the left, another half block, and into an alley. Sara puffed hard but kept running. She had gained somewhat on Dad when she saw him dive into the bushes at the side of the alley, landing on his stomach. His outstretched hand disappeared into the bushes.

About the time Sara reached Dad's side, puffing hard, he let out a loud yelp. Then he withdrew his hand from the bushes, still holding Tina's back foot. And Sara smelled that awful smell!

Sara looked down to see Tina chewing on Dad's hand. Dad's eyes were closed tightly, and in spite of the fox's sharp teeth, he hung on. "Sara," he gritted through his teeth, "can you make that thing stop biting me?"

Sara finally came to her senses and grabbed Tina up in her arms, stink and all. The fox settled right down and cuddled close. Sara held her pet firmly, even though she felt almost ready to throw up.

Dad struggled to his feet and gave Sara a

sickly grin, "Sorry," he mumbled. "But if I hadn't tackled her, we would have lost her for sure." Sara and Dad retraced their steps to Grandma's house. Everyone they met moved completely off the sidewalk to let them pass.

She gave Tina a soapy bath in an old tub in Grandma's backyard. Grandpa stood back several feet and watched Sara cleaning the animal. "When you're through there, I'll give your dad a bath in that water. And you had better be next after that." He grinned, and Sara knew he wasn't mad at her or her pet.

"Are you sure your pet is worth all the trouble she causes?" Grandma asked after everyone was cleaned up. Dad had bathed and dressed in Grandpa's cords and shirt. Sara wore an old pair of Grandma's jeans and a light sweater, even though they were a little short.

"Of course Tina's worth it!" Sara said. "She's giving us a little sample of heaven. We'll have all kinds of animals in heaven, you know. They won't be afraid of us, either."

"And they won't even stink," Derek said. "Hey, you know what Tina means?" he asked Grandma. Then he proudly answered his own question. "It means an old scab worm."

"Derek! It does not! It means—uh—well, it means she's a fat little tub."

Grandma shook her silver head. "No, dear, *Tina* is the nickname for *Christina*, which means 'tiny.' *Christina* means 'a tiny, Christlike girl.'" She shook her head. "It might be French—or Spanish, I'm not sure."

Sara hugged Grandma. "You can't guess how glad I am to hear that," she whispered into Grandma's ear. "Now, Derek, you can forget about the scabby worm, OK?"

The next afternoon, Derek couldn't find his teddy bear and couldn't take his nap without it. Sara and Mom looked all over the house before giving up. "You must have taken Teddy outside," Mom said. "Teddy bears never run away by themselves."

"I didn't," Derek said tearfully. "Teddy was tired this morning and stayed in bed. I haven't seen him since."

Sara went outside and looked everywhere Derek had been. She felt certain he had left his tattered friend lying around somewhere. But she found nothing. Finally, Derek dropped tearfully off to sleep.

Teddy was still missing at suppertime. "I

can't go to bed tonight without Teddy, Daddy," Derek said after everyone finished eating.

Dad tousled Derek's blond hair. "You still have the cats. Why aren't the cats enough?"

"Because."

"Are you sure you've looked all through the house?" Dad asked Mom.

Mom nodded. "It isn't in the house."

Dad jumped to his feet. "OK, everyone outside. The one who finds Teddy gets a special treat."

"Even if it's me, Daddy?" Derek asked.

Dad grabbed Derek and tossed him into the air. "Especially if it's you. After all, you're the one who's been getting along without that bad bear, aren't you?"

Derek ran away laughing.

Everyone looked everywhere: behind shrubs, in the flower beds, in the garden, in the small ornamental trees. But no one found the bear.

"I guess we'll have to look farther," Dad said. "Mom and I will look in the berry and grape patches; Sara and Derek, you look in the wild area."

"Let's ask God to help us find it," Sara said. The whole family knelt on the back lawn, held hands, and told their kind heavenly Father how much Derek loved his teddy and asked Him to help them find it.

"We'll find Teddy now," Derek said happily. Sara and Derek ran out into the tall, dry grass. "I'm going to look around the manzanita bushes, Derek," Sara said. "You look in the grass."

As Sara searched in the waist-high bushes, she noticed a movement on the low-hanging oak limb. Walking slowly toward it, she saw Tina disappear into the treehouse. What was that she had in her mouth?

*Sara, Derek, and Tina slept
in the back seat after their camping trip.*

# CHAPTER

## 7

# Tina Goes Camping

Sara ran to the tree and climbed up the board ladder. When she stepped into the treehouse, Tina looked up in surprise, then dropped the sock she had just carried in. She ran in small circles around Sara, whining. Sara sat down on the rough floor, and Tina jumped into her lap.

Sara stroked the happy little animal. "Why are you so excited, Tina? I haven't been gone. And you've been gone only a little while."

Sara petted Tina as she looked around. There was her missing sweater, both of Derek's sneakers, the cat-food dish, Mom's weeder, and the book she had lost! And Teddy!

Sara jumped up, dumping Tina on the floor, and ran to the window. "I found Teddy," she shouted. "I found the bear."

In a few minutes, Derek, Mom, and Dad crowded into the treehouse with Tina and Sara. Mom picked up the things one by one. "She's a real thief." Mom said. "She's been bringing everything out here that she can carry."

"She saw us carrying things out here, so she did it too," Derek said.

Time flew by, and almost before Sara knew it, it was time for their vacation. The family packed the tent, sleeping bags, camp stove, and lantern into the old green station wagon and headed for Canada. Two days later, Dad slowed the car. "Look, kids, we're coming up to customs. This is the border between our country and Canada."

Two uniformed men approached the car, both smiling. "Do you have any firearms?" one of them asked.

Dad shook his head. "We don't use guns. We do have some cameras."

"That's fine. How long are you planning to stay?"

"About ten days," Dad said.

The man stepped back and waved them through. "Have a nice vacation," he called as Dad drove into Canada.

A couple of hours later, the family drove tent pegs into the ground and set up the tent in a woodsy campground in the Canadian Rocky Mountains. Then Sara and Derek carried sleeping bags and suitcases into the tent while Dad and Mom made supper.

Tina ran in large circles around the camp, sniffing at every tree and plant until Mom called everyone for supper. Sara fed Tina, and after worship by the campfire, the little fox was more than ready to curl up inside Sara's sleeping bag with her.

Early the next morning, Sara and Tina crept out to look around the campground. A twig snapped about 50 feet away, and Sara saw three deer—a mother, a fawn, and another doe—grazing in a small, sunny clearing. "Tina," Sara whispered as the fox flattened herself on the ground, then wiggled closer to the grazing deer. "Come back here, Tina."

She held her breath when Tina ignored her call and kept crawling. When the deer noticed

Tina, they jerked their heads high, with their ears up. The mother deer walked slowly to meet her. Tina stood quietly while the doe approached. The fox and deer gazed into each other's eyes, then their noses slowly touched.

Sara watched the curious fox and the beautiful deer sniffing each other. Then she hurried quietly to the tent. "Come see Tina with the deer," she whispered.

Derek burst from the tent. "Where?" he shouted. "Where are the deer?"

Sara popped her hand over his mouth, took him to where he could see the clearing, and pointed. Tina and the mother deer still stood quietly, nose to nose.

After breakfast, the family went to see Lake Louise. On the way, they saw a herd of elk grazing in the lush grass beside the road. They drove through a herd of buffalo. A few miles farther down the road, they saw several cars stopped. Dad pulled up behind them. Then Sara saw why! A black bear stood beside the road on its hind feet.

Early the next morning, a strange sound awakened the family. *Ow, ow, owoo!* "Something's howling," Dad said. "I'm not sure what it is."

*Ow, ow, owoo!* Now it sounded as if the animal was standing right outside their tent. Then another one howled, farther away. Sara felt shivers going up and down her backbone, even though she was cozy warm. But with a quick wiggle, Tina zipped out of the sleeping bag. The little animal crawled under the zipped tent door and vanished.

Sara jumped up. "Help quick, Dad! Tina just ran outside!"

The mournful howl came again. Sara felt terrified, but she unzipped the tent door and stepped outside. In the grayness of early morning, she thought every tree trunk moved. But she saw neither Tina nor the howling animals. Finally, Dad crawled from the tent, with Mom and Derek following. The animals didn't howl again.

"Do you think Tina went to chase the animals away or to hide?" Sara asked.

"Maybe those were foxes," Derek said. "Maybe she wanted to meet them."

Dad shook his head. "I don't think foxes howl like that, son. They were either wolves or coyotes. Tina ran to hide."

"Wolves! We'd better pack up and get out of here," Mom said.

"Not without Tina," Sara said.

"Not at all," Dad added. "They were probably coyotes, but whatever they were, they're not going to bother us. Come on, we'll make some breakfast. Maybe Tina will smell our food and come running back."

But Tina wasn't there when breakfast was over. After searching through the campground, the family went on to see more of the sights and animals. "Don't worry," Dad said. "I'm sure Tina will be here when we get back."

But she wasn't. Sara headed right out to search again. She came back empty-handed. "I looked all over the campground and called as loudly as I could," Sara said. "I know she would have come if she had heard me. She always does."

"I'm really sorry about Tina," Mom said. "This camping trip should be a special time for you, not a time to worry."

"Let's pray for Tina to come back," Derek said. Four sincere prayers went up for Tina's safe return, and Sara kept watching for her pet to burst into the campsite. But she finally crawled into her sleeping bag alone. Light snores began as everyone fell asleep. Sara felt lonelier than ever. Huddled in her sleeping bag, she listened fearfully to the night sounds— an owl hooting, crickets chirping, trees creaking, and twigs snapping.

But Sara couldn't help smiling as she remembered the silly, funny, loving things her pet had done all summer. *Thank You, God, for letting me have Tina*, she prayed silently. *She's taught me to love You more. She's taught me to care more about animals too. Please keep her safe and bring her back to me. I love her so much.*

Sara kept thinking and listening for little feet scratching at the tent door. Finally she slept.

When she woke up the next morning, she still felt sad. In fact, she didn't feel like getting up and going anywhere. *Maybe I'll just stay right here all day*, she thought. Then she noticed an extra-warm spot on her back. Spinning over, she found a little ball of red fur inside her sleeping bag. It was Tina, crowded as close to Sara as she could get.

Sara grabbed the fox and held her close. She

kissed the dainty little face. And cried. But they were tears of joy. "Mom! Dad! Wake up! Tina's back!"

Sara enjoyed the rest of the camping trip, with Tina either under her arm or at her feet. But finally it was time to go home. Sara, Derek, and Tina slept in the back seat with their heads on pillows as they drove south through Canada. Late in the afternoon, Dad stopped at customs before entering the United States.

"Good afternoon, sir, are you carrying any guns?" the man asked.

"No, sir, just a tired family."

Then the man got a shocked look on his face. He pointed into the back seat. "What do you have back there? Is that a fox?"

Dad glanced over his shoulder and grinned. "Yes, that's Tina, the red fox."

The man's face took on a troubled look. "But you can't bring wild animals into the United States."

Dad only smiled wider. "Why not? We took her into Canada *from* the United States."

"You couldn't have. It's not allowed."

Sara began to get worried. What if they tried to make her leave Tina in Canada?

*Tina, the Really Rascally Red Fox*

# CHAPTER

# 8

# Tina's Baby

*Tina can't stay in Canada,* Sara shouted to herself. *She's my pet. She wouldn't even know how to take care of herself.* She snatched Tina up in her arms and held her tight. "We did bring her to Canada with us," she called from the back seat. "She's my special pet, sir."

The man leaned into the car and took a good look. "How long have you folks been in Canada?"

"Ten days," Dad answered.

The man shook his head. "I'll have to admit, the fox looks too tame to have been in captivity only ten days."

"She's not in captivity," Sara said. "She's never been in captivity. We've had her since she was a tiny little baby, and she goes where she wants, whenever she wants."

The man looked troubled. "I'm really not allowed to let anyone bring in a wild animal." Then his face brightened. "Say," he said, with a wide smile. "Do you have any proof that you took the fox into Canada with you?"

Dad and Mom looked at each other. "I don't know how we could prove it," Mom started to say. Then she snapped her fingers. "Could we call our veterinarian? Tina had pneumonia when she was tiny. I'm sure he would remember her."

After the telephone call, the customs agent let Tina through. Sara hugged her pet close. "We almost lost you in the campground, then we almost lost you at the border. I'm glad we're going home!"

Several days later, Sara and Derek were playing old records in the treehouse when they saw their little red fox running toward them up the long, hanging limb. Tina climbed into the treehouse and dropped something at Sara's feet. Then she sat back and watched Sara. The fox looked for all the world as though she had brought Sara a gift.

Sara leaned over and looked at Tina's "gift."

"It looks like a little rat or a mole," Sara said, drawing back.

"It's wet and yucky," Derek said. "Don't touch it."

"Don't worry. I'm not going to." Sara turned to Tina. "Take your garbage somewhere else, Tina." She gave the fox a pat on the head. "I know I can't stop you from hunting, but please don't bring your catches to me."

Just then, Sara saw the sloppy, wet, gray thing move. She jumped back and put her arm in front of Derek. "That thing's alive, Derek," she hissed. "Stay back."

But Tina didn't stay back. She nuzzled the small animal and whimpered softly.

Sara and Derek watched breathlessly. Sara wanted to take the little thing away from Tina and release it while it was still alive, but she wasn't brave enough to touch it.

Then Tina's little pink tongue came out, and began licking the animal. A moment later, the tiny creature lifted its head.

"Sara, that's not a mole!" Derek cried, pointing. "That's a kitten."

Sure enough, tiny ears stood up from the

wobbly head. Blue eyes peered at the fox from a tiny face. Sara dropped to her knees to watch. Tina kept licking the kitten until its fur looked almost dry.

Sara looked at her small brother. "It's darling, Derek. It's so cute." She scooped the helpless little animal into her left hand and petted it with one finger. Tina stood with her front feet in Sara's lap, watching the kitten closely.

"Let's take it into the house," Derek said. He picked up the kitten and carried it down the board steps.

Sara followed, carrying Tina in her arms.

"Look, Mommy," Derek called as the little procession trailed into the family room. "Tina had a baby!"

That brought Mom in a hurry. Derek laid the tiny bundle of fur in her hand. Mom sat down on the couch, and Tina stood at her side, licking the kitten.

Mom looked from Sara to Derek. "This isn't Tina's baby," she said. "Where did it come from?"

Derek nodded his head up and down wildly. "Yes, it is, Mommy," he said. "Tina brought it to us in the treehouse. It's her baby."

Mom put her arm around the little boy. "This is a kitten, son. Cats have kittens. Foxes have baby foxes. And people have baby people. Jesus made it that way."

"Well, it's hers, anyway."

Sara nodded. "She thinks it's hers, Mom. Hey, can I use Tina's bottle to feed the kitten?"

"Yes. Remember how we fixed Tina's formula? Let's see if the kitten will drink that." The kitten sucked eagerly on the soft nipple. Its little feet pumped against Sara's hand as it drank, purring loudly.

When Dad came home, he didn't take the kitten's arrival so well. "What are you going to do when Tina hauls in the rest of the litter?" he asked.

Derek's blue eyes grew wide. "No, Daddy, she won't. She just had one baby."

Dad hauled Derek onto his lap. "How would you know that, son?"

"Because—because," Derek took another breath and tried again. "She just had one baby."

Dad laughed and hugged Derek. "All right, she just had one. But we already have two spoiled cats, one old dog, a tame fox, and two wild kids. We simply can't take in another cat."

"What are we going to do with it, then?" Sara asked. "It can't even walk."

"Jesus wants us to be kind to animals, Daddy," Derek said. "That's what you said."

Everyone looked into the little box on the floor. Tina lay in the box, curled around the kitten. The kitten slept, but Tina's bright eyes watched Sara.

After a few moments, Dad cleared his throat. "Do you think it could sleep on the patio?"

Sara carried the box to the patio, with Tina following close behind. "Are you going to sleep out here too, Sara?" Derek asked.

"I don't think Dad will let me. I'll probably have to get up in the night and feed it, though."

Sara went out and fed the kitten and covered it with soft cloths before she went to bed. Then she scooted between her cool sheets and held up the covers so Tina could sleep close. But the little fox couldn't settle down. Finally, Tina jumped out of bed and ran from the room. A few minutes later, she started yapping.

*Dad will pitch her out if I don't get her quieted,* Sara thought as she ran down the hall.

She found Tina waiting for her at the sliding-glass door in the family room. "You come to bed, Tina." Sara carried the little fox back to bed and climbed in with her. Sara barely got situated when Tina jumped out of bed and ran from the room again. Then the yapping began—even louder this time.

Finding the fox at the glass door again, it hit Sara like a cup of cold water. Tina wanted to be with the kitten! Sara slid the door open about six inches, and Tina zapped through.

"I'm not so sure I'm happy about the kitten," Sara said the next morning, after she told Mom and Dad about sleeping alone. "Tina was all curled up with the kitten when I took the bottle out in the night."

"She has to keep it warm," Derek said. Derek spent a lot of time with the kitten the following days, and so did Tina. "I'm naming the kitty 'Streaky,'" he announced one evening at the supper table.

"Why Streaky?" Mom asked.

"Because I see little streaks coming in his grey fur."

"OK, I guess he's Streaky," Dad agreed.

Streaky ate like an elephant and grew almost like one too. He drank as many bottles of milk as Sara would take to him. And Tina slept with him every night. Sara missed having Tina sleep with her. She would have brought Tina and her baby in and slept with them both, but Dad was sure Streaky needed to be an outside cat.

Tina kept the kitten nice and clean, so Sara didn't have to worry about that. One afternoon, Sara sent Derek to find the kitten so it could have it's milk. He came shrieking back to the house, his arms empty. "Streaky's gone!"

*Sara returns Tina's "pet" chickens.*

# CHAPTER

# 9

# Tina Steals Chickens

Sara raced outside. "He's around somewhere," she told Derek. "We'll find him." In a little while, they found the kitten, playing with Tina in the grape vineyard. Before they could say anything, Tina stood on her feet, snagged several grapes, and laid them in front of the kitten. Streaky ignored the grapes and started to wander off.

Tina jumped into the vine again and came down with a cluster of grapes in her mouth. She caught up with Streaky and put them on the ground in front of him. He stretched and walked around them, barely glancing in their direction. Tina jumped in front of the cat and pawed playfully at the grapes.

Sara ran and squatted beside Tina. "What are you trying to do, Tina?" she asked. She pulled Tina to her and gave the fox a quick hug. Then she picked up the grapes and held them to Tina. Tina gobbled them up.

That night, Sara told Mom and Dad about Tina trying to feed grapes to Streaky.

"She really thinks Streaky is a fox," Mom said.

"A gray fox," Derek added.

"It's pretty neat the way God made mothers love and care for their babies," Dad said. "No matter what kind of animal you name, the mother loves her babies a lot. And He shows the mothers how to care for the babies."

"Yeah," Sara agreed. "Even when the baby isn't really hers."

Before long, it was time for school to start. Sara liked school, but she missed spending time with Tina. Several days later, Sara came home from school to find Tina in the backyard with two big red hens. As Sara watched, Tina ran around the hens, stopping them from leaving the lawn. Tina moved quietly, but she seemed to think that the lawn was the chickens' pen, and it was her job to keep them in it.

The chickens didn't get excited, but Sara did. "Mom, where did these chickens come from?"

Mom stepped outside. "What chickens?" she started to ask. Then she saw them. "Oh! I don't know," she said, blowing a curl off her forehead. "I've never seen them before. How do you suppose they got in our backyard?"

Sara glanced at Tina, who was still running in front of the hens every time they tried to step off the lawn. "I guess Tina brought them home. Mom, this is worse than bringing home the kitten. You can't go around stealing people's chickens."

Mom thought for a moment. "Well, they can't belong to our neighbors across the street. They don't keep any chickens."

"Knowing Tina," Sara said, "I think she brought these chickens through the woods. I suppose I'd better go see what I can find."

With that, Sara started toward the woods at the back of the yard. Tina wanted to go with her. She ran after Sara a little way, then looked over her shoulder at the chickens and ran back. After running back and forth two or three times, Tina decided that the chickens needed her more than Sara did. She lay down near the chickens and rested her nose on her paws. Tina looked relaxed, but Sara knew she would never let those chickens leave the lawn. *If Tina stays here, those chickens will be here when I get back*, she decided.

Tramping through the woods behind her home, Sara kept asking herself, *Who do these woods belong to?* She kept going until she found a clearing with some houses that faced another road. Walking along the back border of those yards, she saw one yard with about a dozen red chickens just like Tina's.

*But these chickens are behind strong wire fences*, Sara thought. *How could Tina have gotten them out?* But there were no chickens at the other houses, so Sara decided that the house with the chickens must be the place Tina had visited.

Gathering up her courage, Sara went to the back door and knocked.

A big man with a big stomach answered the door. "Whatta ya want? And what are ya doing at my back door?" he asked, without a smile. "I don't like people snooping around my place."

Sara felt her mouth go dry. "I live on the next road through those woods," she answered, pointing behind her. "Are you missing some chickens?"

"How would I know?"

The man's scowling face frightened Sara. "I have two strange hens in my backyard, sir," she squeaked.

He peered out toward his pen but didn't offer to go check. "Toss them inside the fence," he growled. Then he slammed the door in Sara's face.

Sara turned and raced home. She told Mom about the rude man. "If he doesn't know, how does he expect us to?" Mom asked. "But since you didn't find anyone else with chickens, you may as well do as he said."

Tina jumped around unhappily when Sara captured Tina's private flock of chickens. When Sara had both hens under her arms, Mom took Tina inside the house.

By the time Sara walked back through the woods, she knew what she was going to do. She didn't ring the doorbell. She just tossed the chickens over the fence. *Just like that man said to do*, she said to herself as she watched the hens flutter to the ground. They walked right over to the water dish as if they knew exactly where they were.

The next afternoon, when Sara came home from school, she took one look at the yard and felt her heart drop into her shoes. "No, Tina!" But there was the fox, guarding her two chickens on the lawn again.

The little fox looked up at Sara, her eyes shining, as if to say, "See, I brought them back for you."

Sara returned to the chicken yard. When the chickens landed in the pen, they strutted around exactly like the others. *I wonder if Tina got the same two chickens both days*, she thought, shaking her head. When she got home, she shook her finger in Tina's bright little face. "Now don't you do that anymore."

That night, Sara prayed for God to protect her bad little fox and for Him to teach Tina not to bother the chickens.

But the next day, Tina had her flock on the back lawn again. *Why God? Why didn't You stop her?* she asked silently. Then she sighed and ran to change her clothes. As she was buttoning her shirt, she heard—no, she felt—

a voice speaking to her.

*I'm watching your pet, Sara, but it's your job to stop her from stealing chickens.*

Sara believed that God had spoken to her and that He would protect Tina. *I have to stop Tina from rustling those chickens*, she decided. *I don't want to tie her up, but how else can I control her?*

Sara felt like crying the next day when she found Tina watching over her chickens again.

Grabbing a hen under each arm, she ran through the woods to the rude man's place. Tina was right behind her.

As she dropped the chickens inside the fence, the man appeared beside her. And he was mad. "I've been watching you messing around with my chickens, kid. And I'm telling you right now, if I see you or that fox again, I'll turn my big red dog loose. And believe me, neither of you wants to meet him!"

*Tina, the Really Rascally Red Fox*

# CHAPTER

# *10*

# A New Enemy and a New Friend

A cold shiver shot through Sara. *A dog might kill Tina*, she thought. "Y-y-yes sir. We'll stay away from your place." Sara took off as fast as she could go with Tina running right beside her.

"We'll think of something," Dad said when Sara told him about the chickens and the mean man. "You'll just have to keep her busy around here. Maybe she'll forget about those chickens."

"Come on, Tina. Time for bed," Sara said later. As she pulled back the sheets and crawled into bed, she prayed. *Dear Father, are you still watching over my baby? Could You show me how to make her quit bothering the chickens? Thank you, God. I love you.*

As Sara pulled the covers up, Tina ran out of the room down the hall to the patio door. Sara struggled up. *She probably needs to go out to potty.* "Do what you have to do quickly," she told the fox. Tina did what she had to do. But it was't what Sara was expecting. Tina looked at Sara for a moment, then trotted off into the woods.

"Tina, come back here," Sara shouted into the dark night. But Tina didn't return that night at all. The next morning though, she was waiting at the door for her breakfast.

"Are we picking grapes today?" Dad asked as he cut his waffle.

"I'd like to," Mom answered. "And I need some help." So the whole family headed for the grape vines after breakfast. Tina joined them.

An hour passed, and many flat boxes of grapes lay on the back lawn. "How long do we have to pick?" Derek whined. "I filled my bucket two times."

"Until they're all picked, sport," Dad said with a smile. "Don't you want to help us make grape juice?"

Derek rubbed a blue-stained hand over his eyes, but before he could answer, a big racket came from the woods. Loud yapping grew closer, followed by barking and growling. Dad, Mom, Sara, and Derek all rushed toward the sounds.

Tina burst into the clearing, yapping sadly. A big red dog chased close behind, barking loudly, it's jaws snapping at Tina's tail.

Sara stood wide-eyed, too scared to move. But old Duke struggled to his feet and got between the dog and Tina. The dog crashed right into Duke. With a deep roar, Duke grabbed the other dog's neck and started chewing.

Yelping like a puppy, the dog twisted loose and ran for home. Duke followed for a few steps, then lay down. Tina jumped into Sara's arms. Every muscle in her tiny body was trembling.

Sara sat on a bucket, cuddling her pet. "She's been to see those chickens again, Dad. What are we going to do?"

Dad grinned. "Your chicken problem is solved, Sara. Tina won't forget that dog. She won't go back."

As she carried Tina back to the house, Sara had a sudden thought. *God answered my prayer! Tina was scared, but not hurt. Thank You, Father*, she prayed silently. *You always answer my prayers in the very best way.*

After that, Tina began spending more and more time in the woods. But she always came when Sara called. One day, Sara came home from school to find Derek waiting. "Come see what I found," he said, pulling her toward the back door.

Sara shrugged away. "I have homework to do first."

"Sara, come now," he insisted.

With a sigh, Sara followed her brother through the woods to a small hill. He walked part of the way around and pointed down. "See?"

Sara saw a hole, about ten inches around, in the side of the hill. "What does this hole have to do with anything?" she asked.

Derek jabbed his finger at it again. "Look inside," he whispered.

Sara leaned down and peered into the long, dark tunnel. After a moment, her eyes got used to the dark, and she could see a small reddish-looking ball about six feet inside. It was Tina, curled up asleep!

"Come, Tina," Sara called. The fox exploded from the hole and jumped into Sara's arms.

"I knew you would want to see," Derek said as they walked home. Sara nodded and smiled as she carried Tina in her arms.

That night, Sara and Derek told Mom and Dad about Tina sleeping in the hill. "She's learning to be nocturnal (nock-turn-ull)," Dad said.

"That means she sleeps during the day instead of at night," Mom explained.

Sara checked in the encyclopedia and found that foxes are truly nocturnal animals. "See," she told Derek, "they sometimes dig dens seventy-five feet long, with different chambers for sleeping, storing their food, and playing."

"They have bedrooms, kitchens, and family rooms," Derek decided.

Sara took a deep breath. "Dad, does this mean that Tina is getting wild?"

Dad shook his head. "I don't know. She could be."

When the weather turned rainy, Dad let Streaky move into the house and sleep with Sara. With Tina staying out every night now, Streaky helped Sara not be so lonely.

One night, a high yapping woke Sara, and she ran to the sliding glass door. Tina stood outside, rain dripping from her beautiful red fur. When she saw Sara, she ran in circles, yapping again.

Sara slid the door open. "Come in, Tina," she said quietly. "I'ln get a towel and dry you off."

But Tina didn't come in. She ran back and forth across the ground again.

"What do you want?" Sara asked. Tina ran in the direction of the woods, then ran back. When Sara didn't move, Tina ran back toward the woods again, looking back over her shoulder at her friend.

"I suppose I'll have to go," Sara muttered. She stepped out to follow Tina into the wet night. The moon peeped out between clouds to light the backyard a little.

Sara walked along after her fox. But before she got to the woods, Sara stopped. Another small animal stood in the shadows under the trees. Sara could barely see it, until its golden eyes reflected the moonlight. Then as the sharp little face turned, she saw pointed ears standing straight up.

Tina ran up to the animal and jumped over

it. Then she raced around it in circles like she wanted to play a game. But the other animal ignored Tina. Its bright eyes followed Sara's every movement.

The next morning, Sara told everyone what had happened. "It was another fox, Dad. I know it was. Tina's going to leave us, isn't she?"

Dad was't sure. "I don't know, Sara. Either that, or she may stay nearby and bring you baby foxes in the spring. Remember, though, Tina takes her orders straight from God. Whatever she does will be right for her."

―――――

Tina did go back to the wild. Sara missed her very much, but she never forgot the fun she had had with her pet fox. She still thanks God that she was able to have such a loving, interesting pet.

# THE SHOEBOX MYSTERY SERIES

### The Missing Combination Mystery

If only they could find the missing combination to the safe so they could unlock the secret inside.Meanwhile, Chris starts feeling jealous about Ryan's sudden popularity with the gang after he rescues Willie from disaster.

### Jenny's Cat-napped Cat

Butterscotch is missing, and is Jenny mad! The trail of clues leads right to DeeDee's cousin Tevin. But her beloved cat is still missing. Jenny learns a lesson in forgiveness when she discovers who really is to blame for the cat-napping.

### The Mysterious Treasure Map

### The Case of the Secret Code